THiS B**OO**k
belongs to:

ATHENEUM BOOKS FOR YOUNG READERS
An imprint of Simon & Schuster Children's Publishing Division
1230 Avenue of the Americas, New York, New York 10020

For information about special discounts for bulk purchases, please contact
Simon & Schuster Special Sales at 1-866-506-1949
or business@simonandschuster.com.
The Simon & Schuster Speakers Bureau can bring authors to your live
event. For more information or to book an event, contact the
Simon & Schuster Speakers Bureau at 1-866-248-3049
or visit our website at www.simonspeakers.com.
Book design by Lauren Rille
The text for this book is set in Skizzors.
The illustrations for this book are rendered in pencil, then colored digitally.
Manufactured in China
1011 SCP
First Edition
2 4 6 8 10 9 7 5 3 1
Library of Congress Cataloging-in-Publication Data
DiPucchio, Kelly S.
Crafty Chloe / Kelly DiPucchio ; illustrated by Heather Ross. — 1st ed.
p. cm.
Summary: Chloe is very good at sewing and crafts and when her best
friend's birthday approaches, she not only creates a fabulous gift, she also
saves the day for a classmate who had been unkind to her.
ISBN 978-1-4424-2123-3 (hardcover)
ISBN 978-1-4424-4390-7 (eBook)
[1. Handicraft—Fiction. 2. Birthdays—Fiction. 3. Gifts—Fiction.] I. Ross, Heather,
ill. II. Title.
PZ7.D6219Cr 2012
[E]—dc22 2010042811

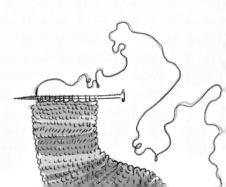

Crafty CHLOE

by
KELLY DiPUCCHIO

illustrations by
HEATHER ROSS

ATHENEUM BOOKS FOR YOUNG READERS
New York London Toronto Sydney New Delhi

This is Chloe.

Chloe isn't very good at sports.

Video games were never her thing.

And when she took dance lessons, she had the grace
of a camel in roller skates.

What Chloe *is* very
good at is making stuff.

She knows that a whole new outfit can be made out of Dad's old shirts,

and that coffee filters make very good flower hats for show-and-tell,

and that *anything* becomes less boring with googly eyes on it.

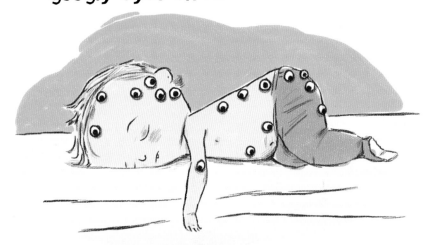

Chloe is very good at making clothes, too.

Her dog, Bert,
pictured here . . .

and here . . .

and here . . .
is very good at
wearing them.

One day Chloe went shopping to look for a

birthday present  for her best friend,

Emma. She looked at diaries,  and

drumsticks,  jewelry boxes,

and jump ropes, but nothing seemed

just right. And then Chloe saw her. Violet.

Of course! All Emma ever talked about

was her Flower Girl dolls. She had all of them

except the new girl, Violet.

Chloe reached for the doll and felt a tap on her shoulder.

She turned around
and there was London . . .

. . . with her arms wrapped around Violet.

"If you're looking for a gift for Emma," she said extra sweetly, "I already found the perfect present!"

Chloe's smile faded. She shrugged, pretending not to care. "That's okay, because I'm going to make her something special that you can't even buy in a store."

London cried in disbelief. She wrinkled up

her nose as if Chloe had just announced she

was going to give Emma a jar of pickles for

her birthday.

Chloe stood there feeling like a dried-up

glue stick. She didn't know *what* to say. "It's

going to be very PURPLE,"

came out of her mouth.

London made a snorty laugh. "Well, good

luck with *that!*"

That afternoon Chloe stared hopelessly into
her pile of craft supplies.

A macaroni necklace? Nah.

A coffee mug? Nope.

A sock monkey?
Definitely not.

Nothing she thought of
seemed more perfect than a Violet doll.

Chloe came down for dinner a few hours later covered in blue spots. She placed the get-well card she had made for herself on the table.

Chloe's father raised his eyebrows.

Chloe's mother checked her for a fever.

Chloe's baby brother spit out his green beans.

And Bert, pictured here . . .

and here . . .

and here . . . made faces.

"Make all the faces you like," Chloe groaned. "I have
Chicken Pops and I can't go to the party tomorrow."

"What a shame," her mother said. "Emma's such a good friend, and you'll miss the pony rides."

The pony! Darn. Chloe had forgotten all about the pony. And Emma really *was* a good friend. Luckily for Chloe, her Chicken Pops were the washable kind.

After dinner Chloe went to her room to doodle. Doodling helps her think. Thinking gives her ideas. Some ideas are pretty spectacular and require *lots* of glitter.

Chloe worked late into the night.

Gluing.
And painting.
And sewing.

When she finished, she stood
back and admired her work.
She liked it. But would Emma?

The next day Chloe walked to Emma's house carrying
a very big box. London clicked ahead of her in sparkly heels,
swinging her gift bag.

Click. Click. Click.

TRIP!

London fell.

The gift bag flew.

And Violet flopped . . .

. . . right into a puddle. *SPLASH!*

London grabbed Violet.

London's little dog grabbed Violet too.

London *rrrrroared,*

"DROP IT!"

The dress *rrrrripped.*
And the dog ran.

"*What am I going to do?*" London wailed. "I can't give Emma a *naked* doll!"

More than all the googly eyes in the world, Chloe wanted to say, *Well, good luck with that!* But instead she lifted the lid on her box and she pulled out a perfectly purple dress.

"She can wear this."

London reached for the dress. "*Did you really make this?*" she squealed. "It's adorable!"

Chloe's eyes lit up like rhinestones. "My grandma taught me how to sew," she said proudly.

The girls dressed Violet in her new outfit.

London peeked inside the box. "Whoa! Did you make that, too?"

Chloe nodded again. "Do you think Emma will like it?"

London smiled. "I think she's going to love it!"

And she did.

Do you like to make things too?
Visit me at
craftychloe.com
to learn how to make the
cool crafts featured in this book.
See you there!